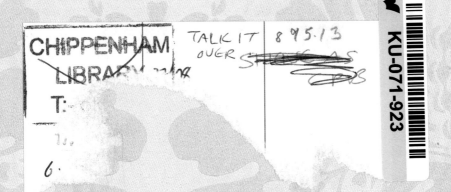

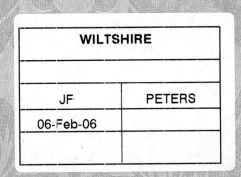

WILTSHIRE	
JF	PETERS
06-Feb-06	

艾莉的秘密日記

Ellie's My Secret Diary

Henriette Barkow & Sarah Garson

Chinese translation by Sylvia Denham

星期日早上 7.30

親愛的日記：

昨晚造了一個惡夢。我一直在跑啊 … 跑的，
一隻龐大的老虎正在追我，我跑得越來越快，
但始終不能逃脫，牠越來越近，跟著 …
我便醒了。我抱著弗珞在臂彎中，
牠令我感到安全 – 牠知道發生什麼事，
我可以告訴牠。常常造惡夢，以前不是這樣的。
我以前有很多朋友 – 例如莎拉和珍妮。
莎拉叫我一起去商店購物，但是 …
自從**她**來了之後，學校便像**地獄**一樣。

我憎恨 憎恨 **憎恨**她!!!

Dear Diary

Had a bad dream last night.
I was running ... and running.
There was this huge
tiger chasing me.
I was running faster and faster but
I couldn't get away.
It was getting closer and then ...
I woke up.

I held Flo in my arms. She makes me feel safe
- she knows what's going on. I can tell her.

Keep having bad dreams.
Didn't used to be like that.
I used to have loads of friends – like Sara and Jenny.
Sara asked me to go to the shops but...

School's been HELL
since SHE came.

I hate hate
HATE her!!!

Sunday evening 20.15

Dear Diary

Went to Grandad's.
Lucy came and we climbed the big tree.
We played pirates.
School 2morrow.
Don't think I can face it.
Go to school and
see HER!

SHE'll be waiting. I KNOW she will.

Even when she isn't there I'm scared
she'll come round a corner.
Or hide in the toilets like a bad smell.
Teachers never check what's going
on in there!

If __ONLY__ I didn't have to go.

Flo thinks I'll be ok.

親愛的日記：

去了祖父處。露絲來了，
我們一起爬那棵大樹，
我們也玩海盜遊戲。明天要上學，
我想我無法面對，
往學校和見到**她**。

她會等著，**我知道**她會，即使她不在，
我也害怕她會在拐角處走出來，
或者像臭氣般躲藏在廁所內，
老師從來都不會到那裏查察在那裏發生的事。

要是我不用上學就好了，

弗珞認爲我會沒事的。

又造那個惡夢了，
不過這次是**她**追我，我嘗試逃跑，
但是她走得越來越近，她的手剛剛觸到我的肩膀 …
跟著我便醒了。

我覺得很不舒服，但我強迫自己吃早餐，
所以媽媽沒有發覺有什麼不對。
不能告訴媽媽 – 這會令事情更糟。
不能告訴任何人，他們會覺得我軟弱，
但是我並不軟弱。

問題是<u>那個女孩</u>和**她**對我所做的事情。

Monday morning 7.05

I had that dream again.
Only this time it was HER who was chasing
me. I was trying to run away but she kept
getting closer and her hand was just on my
shoulder ... then I woke up.

I feel sick but I made myself eat
breakfast, so mum won't
think anything's up.
Can't tell mum – it'll just
make it worse.
Can't tell anyone.
They'll think I'm soft
and I'm not.
It's just <u>that girl</u>
and what SHE does to me.

Monday evening 20.30

Dear Diary

SHE was there. Waiting.
Just round the corner from school where nobody could
see her. SHE grabbed my arm and twisted it behind
my back.
Said if I gave her money she wouldn't hit me.
I gave her what I had. I didn't want to be hit.
"I'll get you tomorrow!" SHE said and pushed me over
before she walked off.
It hurt like hell. She ripped my favourite trousers!

Told mum I fell over. She sewed them up.
I feel like telling Sara or Jenny but they
won't understand!!

Glad I've got you and
Flo to talk to.

星期一晚上 20.30

親愛的日記：

她在那裏，等待著，
就在學校附近，那裏沒有人會看到她。**她**抓住我的手臂，
將它扭到我的背後，她說如果我給她錢，她便不會打我，
我於是把我所有的錢都給她，我不想被她打啊。

「我明天會找你！」**她**說，
並把我推倒後才走開，
那實在痛得厲害，
連我最喜歡的褲子也被撕破了。

我告訴媽媽我跌倒了，
她替我把褲子縫補好。
我很想告訴莎拉或珍妮，
但是她們是不會明白的，

好在可以向你和弗珞傾訴。

昨晚睡不著，
只是躺在那裏，害怕到睡不著，
害怕我會再造那個惡夢。
她會等著我，

爲什麼她總是挑剔**我**？我沒有對她做過任何事。
一定是睡著了，因爲媽媽跟著便叫醒我。

吃不下早餐，把它給了森姆，
因此媽媽不會注意到。

Couldn't sleep last night.
Just lay there. Too scared to go to sleep.
Too scared I'd have that dream again.
SHE'll be waiting for me. Why does she always
pick on ME? I haven't done anything to her.
Must have dropped off, cos next thing
mum was waking me.

Couldn't eat breakfast.
Gave it to Sam so mum wouldn't notice.

她跟著我離開學校
－又高大又兇惡。
她扯我的頭髮，很想大叫，
但我不想令她有滿足感。

「你有錢給我嗎？」**她**向著我唾罵。我搖頭。
「那我就要這個，」**她**怒喝著，
然後奪去我的體育袋，「直至你把錢給我。」

我真渴望能打她一頓！真想在她的肥臉上送上一拳！
我可以做什麼呢？我不能打她，因爲她比我強大。

我不能向爸爸或媽媽索錢，
因爲他們會想知道要錢的原因。

SHE followed me out of school – all big and ~~tuff~~ tough.
SHE pulled my hair. Wanted to scream but I didn't want
to give her the satisfaction.
"You got my money?" SHE spat at me.
Shook my head. "I'll have this," SHE snarled, snatching
my PE bag, "til you give it to me."
I'd love to give it to her! Feel like punching her fat face!
What can I do? I can't hit her cos she's bigger than me.

I can't ask mum
or dad for the money
cos they'll want to
know what it's for.

日記，我做了壞事，

真的很壞！

如果媽媽知道了，我不知她會做什麼，
但我卻會有很大的麻煩－肯定會。

昨晚我看見媽媽的手袋在桌上，
那時就只有我一人，於是我便取了五英鎊。

我會盡快把它放回的，
我會將我的零用錢儲存起來，
我更會嘗試賺一些錢。

　　　希望媽媽不會發覺，

　　　她會很惱怒的！

Diary I've done something bad.
Really bad!

If mum finds out I don't know what she'll do.
But I'll be in big trouble - for sure.

Last night I saw mum's purse on the table.
I was on my own and so I took £5.

← flo

I'll put it back as soon as I can.
I'll save my pocket money.
I'll try and earn some money.

Hope mum doesn't miss it.

She'll go mad!

今天是我一生人中最差的一天!!

第一 – 被譴責，因爲我沒有體育用品。
第二 – 沒有做我的功課。
第三 – **她**就在側門 – 等候著，她扭我的手臂，
然後把錢拿走，還將我的書包掉到泥堆去。
第四 – **她**想要更多錢。
我不會有更多的錢 …
我已經從媽媽處偷過，
我真的不知道怎麼辦。

真希望我從來沒有
來過這個世界!!

This has been the worst day of my life!!

1st - got told off cos I didn't have my PE things.
2nd - hadn't done my homework.
3rd - SHE was by the side gate - waiting.
She twisted my arm and took the money.
Threw my bag in the mud.
4th - SHE wants more.
I can't get more...
I've already stolen from mum.
I don't know what to do.

Wish I'd never been born!!

我真的不能相信。

媽媽發覺了!!

她想知道有沒有人看到她那五英鎊的紙幣，
我們都說不知道，我還能說什麼呢？

我覺得很不安，認真不安，我最憎恨説謊的。
媽媽說她會送我到學校去，
最低限度我會安全，直至放學爲止。

I can't believe it.
Mum's found out!!

She wanted to know if anybody
had seen her £5 note.
We all said no.
What else could I say?

I feel bad, really bad. I hate lying.
Mum said she's taking me to school.
At least I'll be safe til home time.

On the way to school mum asked me if I took the
money.
She looked so sad.
I had thought of lying but seeing her face
I just couldn't.
I said yes and like a stupid idiot burst into tears.

Mum asked why?
And I told her about the girl and what she'd been
doing to me. I told her how scared I was.
I couldn't stop crying.
Mum held me and hugged me.

When I'd calmed down, she asked,
if there was anyone at school
I could talk to?
I shook my head.
She asked if I would
like her to talk to
my teacher.

媽媽在往學校途中問我有沒有拿走了她的錢，
她好像很悲傷似的，我想過再說謊，
但當我看到她的面孔後，我實在不能夠再說謊，
我於是說是我，
跟著我就好像一個愚蠢的呆子般哭了起來。

媽媽問我爲什麼？
我於是把那個女孩和她對我所做的事告訴媽媽，
告訴她我如何的驚慌害怕，我始終不能停止哭，
媽媽抱著我，擁抱我，當我平靜下來後，

她問我學校內是否有人可以讓我傾訴，
我搖搖頭，她於是問我是否想她跟老師說。

Friday morning 6.35

Dearest Diary

Still woke up real early but

I DIDN'T HAVE THAT DREAM!!

I feel a bit strange. Know she won't be in school - they suspended her for a week. What if she's outside?

My teacher said she did it to others - to Jess and Paul.

I thought she'd only picked on me.
But what happens if she's there?

最親愛的日記

依然很早便起床，但是

我沒有再造那個夢!!

我覺得有點奇怪，我知道她不會在學校
– 他們命令她停學一個星期。
假如她在外面等著，那又怎麼辦？

我的老師說她也曾對其他人這樣
– 對杰西和保羅。

我還以爲她只是挑剔我。
但是如果她在那裏，那便怎麼辦？

她真的不在那裏!!! 我跟一位很友善的姑娘傾談，
她說我隨時都可以跟她談話，
並說如果有任何人欺侮你，你應該嘗試告訴其他人。

我將事情告訴莎拉和珍妮，
莎拉說她在以前的學校也遇到同樣的經歷，
不是錢，而是被一名男孩經常挑剔。

我們會在學校互相照顧，不讓任何人受到欺侮。
可能這樣便會沒事吧。當我回到家時，
媽媽為我預備了我最喜歡吃的晚餐。

Friday evening 20.45

She really wasn't there!!!
I had a talk with a nice lady who said I could talk to
her at any time. She said that if anyone is bullying
you, you should try and tell somebody.
I told Sara and Jenny. Sara said it had happened to her
at her last school. Not the money bit but this boy kept
picking on her.

We're all going to look after each other at school so
that nobody else will get bullied. Maybe it'll be ok.
When I got home mum made my favourite dinner.

親愛的日記

不用上學！　　　沒有造惡夢！

瀏覽了電子網絡一會兒，
那裏有很多有關蠻橫霸道的資料。
我以爲這種事情本來並不尋常，
但原來是經常發生的，
甚至在成年人的世界以及魚類之間也有發生。

你知道備受欺侮的魚會因爲受到壓力以致死亡的嗎？

有各種援助專綫電話以及其他這類的資料供應
– 給人類，不是魚類!!

我希望我早就知道！

Saturday morning 8.50

Dear diary
         No school!   No bad dreams!
Had a look on the net and there was loads about
bullying. I didn't think that it happened often but it
happens all the time! Even to grown-ups and fishes.
Did you know that fishes can die from the stress of
being bullied?
There are all kinds of helplines
and stuff like that
- for people, not fishes!!

I wish I'd known!

星期六晚上 21.05

爸爸帶我和森姆去看電影，
真是十分有趣，我們都大笑一頓。

森姆想知道我爲什麼沒有將發生的事情告訴他，

「我會打她一頓！」他說，
「那麼你也成爲一個欺負別人的小霸王了！」
我告訴他說。

Dad took me and Sam to see a film. It was really funny.
We had such a laugh.
Sam wanted to know why I never told him about what was
going on.
"I would have smashed her face!" he said.
"That would just have made you a bully too!" I told him.

What Ellie found out about bullying:

If you are bullied by anyone in any way IT IS NOT YOUR FAULT!
NOBODY DESERVES TO BE BULLIED!
NOBODY ASKS TO BE BULLIED!

There are many ways in which somebody can be bullied.
Can you name the ways in which Ellie was bullied?
Here is a list of some of the ways children are bullied:
  - being teased
  - being called names
  - getting abusive messages on your mobile phone
  - getting hate mail either on email or by letter
  - being ignored or left out
  - having rumours or lies spread about you
  - being pushed, kicked, shoved or pulled about
  - being hit or punched or hurt physically in any way
  - having your bag or other belongings taken and thrown about
  - being forced to hand over money or your belongings
  - being attacked because of your race, religion or the way you speak or dress

Ellie found that it helped to keep a diary of what was happening to her.
It's a way of keeping a record of dates and times when things occurred.
It's also a way of not bottling everything up. It is important that you try
and tell somebody what is going on.
Maybe you could try talking to a friend who you trust.
Maybe you could try talking to your mum or dad, sister or brother.
Maybe there is a teacher at school who you feel comfortable talking to.
Most schools have an anti-bullying policy and may have somebody
(like the kind lady Ellie mentions in her diary) to talk to.

Here are some of the helplines
and websites that Ellie found:

Helplines:

CHILDLINE 0800 I I I I

KIDSCAPE 020 7730 3300

NSPCC 0808 800 5000

Websites:

In the UK:
www.bbc.co.uk/schools/bullying
www.bullying.co.uk
www.childline.org.uk
www.dfes.gov.uk/bullying
www.kidscape.org.uk/info

In Australia & New Zealand:
www.kidshelp.com.au
www.bullyingnoway.com.au
ww.nobully.org.nz

In the USA & Canada:
www.bullying.org
www.pta.org/bullying
www.stopbullyingnow.com

If you want to read more about bullying there are many excellent books
so just check your library or any good bookshop.

Books in the *Diary Series*:
Bereavement
Bullying
Divorce
Migration

A CIP catalogue record for this book is available
from the British Library

First published 2004 by Mantra Lingua
Global House, 303 Ballards Lane
London N12 8NP
www.mantralingua.com